BuiLDa

THE Re-BicycLeR

by Michael Scotto

illustrated by The Ink Circle

BuiLDa o. BoBo
The Bike Factory Owner

The town of Midlandia was bicycle-crazy! Every bike in town came from the same place: Builda's factory. She made beautiful bikes, and the Midlandians kept her very busy.

"I have a problem," said Sparky. "My front tire popped." That certainly was a problem. Sparky was a firefighter and he needed good tires to ride quickly from place to place.

"**Don't worry,**" replied Builda. "I'll have a brand new bike for you by the end of the week."

It may seem odd to build a brand new bike when the only problem is a popped tire. But in Midlandia, this was quite common. When any little thing broke on a bike, its owner threw the bike away and bought a new one.

Sometimes Midlandians threw away bikes that had nothing wrong with them at all.

Every old bike was put into the garbage dump, which was a huge hole in the ground near the edge of town. "I'm tired of this pink bike," said Beaker, as she rolled it into the dump. "I want a blue one."

Throwing away all of these bikes had always seemed like a waste to Builda. "But it is the way things have always been done," she thought. There had never been a reason to change—until now.

When Builda brought Sparky's bike to the dump, she saw an unusual sight. The dump was full! "No, it's more than full," thought Builda. **"It is overflowing!"**

All sorts of mostly good bikes were tangled in a towering pile. "I have to do something about this," she declared.

But what could she do? "If I dig another dump," thought Builda, "it will just fill up, too. And if we keep on digging dumps, there won't be room for anything else!"

Then, Builda saw a bike in the dump that caught her eye. This bike had a bent frame. "But the tires are fine!" she cried. **Builda had a plan!**

Builda carried both bikes back to her factory and worked through the night. In the morning, she had Sparky visit her.

Sparky rode a few test laps around the factory. "It rides just like my old bike," he told Builda with a beaming smile. **"And it looks just like it, too."**

"That's because it is your old bike," said Builda.

Sparky was confused. "My bike was broken," he replied.

"You only had a popped tire," explained Builda. "The rest of your bike was fine. So, I found another bike with a perfect tire, and I put that tire on your bike."

"What a neat idea!" said Sparky. "It saved a lot of time."

"And if we keep reusing our old bike parts," added Builda, "it will also make a lot less garbage."

"You need to tell everyone about your idea," said Sparky. "You could have Vincent make a poster about it for the town square."

Builda explained everything to Vincent, an artist in town. "Instead of throwing our old bikes away, we can reuse the parts to fix other bikes. How clever!" said Vincent. "I'll definitely make a poster for you—but it needs a title. What do you call this idea?"

Builda told him with pride,
"I call it...re-bicycling!"

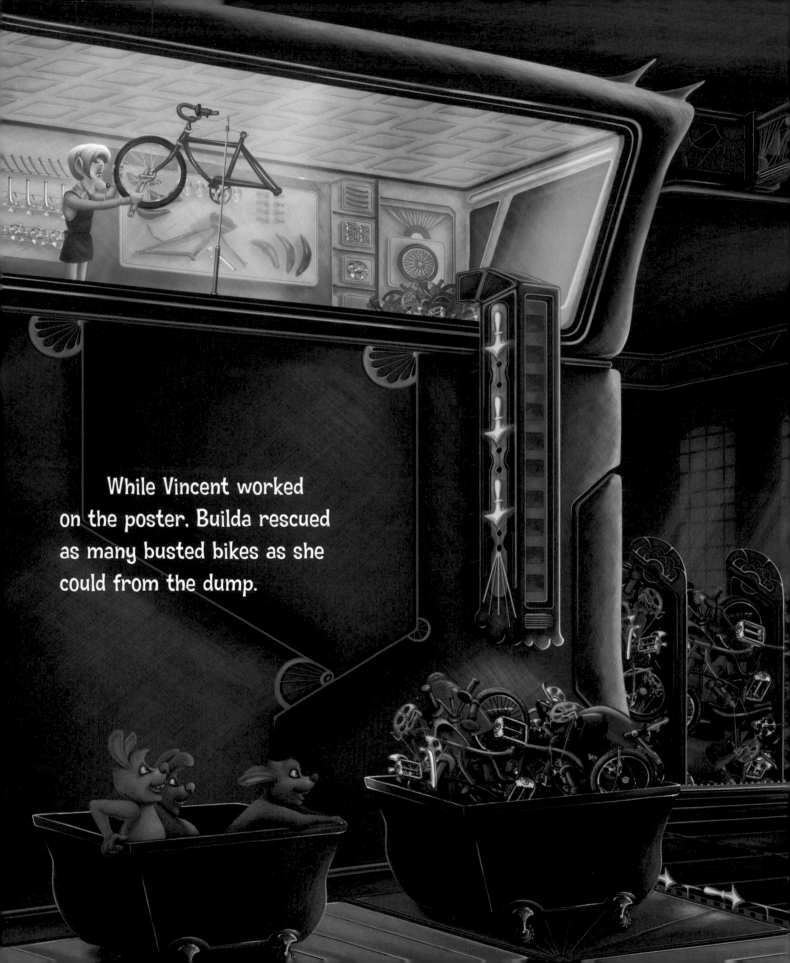

While Vincent worked on the poster. Builda rescued as many busted bikes as she could from the dump.

All through the night, she split the good parts from the bad. She kept the good parts that she could reuse and returned the broken ones to the dump.

Builda went to check on Vincent. "Your poster is almost ready," he said, "but there is one problem. This word...re-bicycling. It's too long to fit on the poster. Can we give your idea a shorter name?"

Builda thought long and hard. Finally, she said, "Why don't we call it **recycling?**"

"Brilliant!" said Vincent. "Recycling is a perfect fit."

Vincent was right—recycling was a perfect fit. Soon, Midlandians began using Builda's idea for more than just bikes.

"Instead of throwing our bottles and cans into the dump," said Beaker, "we can recycle them to make new ones!"

"We can take used paper and recycle it to make new paper!" exclaimed Nueva.

After some time, Chief Tatupu, the leader of Midlandia, visited Builda's factory. "**I have wonderful news,**" he said. "For your idea, recycling, I have come to award you with a great honor: the **Spirit of Midlandia trophy!**"

Builda's eyes grew wide. "I don't know if I deserve that," she stammered.

"Recycling has helped us in so many ways," said Chief.

"It's reduced the trash that we produce and helped save our resources," said Sparky.

"But best of all," noted Vincent, "it has made Midlandia a cleaner and more beautiful place."

"All that happened because of my little idea?" asked Builda.

Chief smiled. "We are having a ceremony for you tomorrow evening. I hope you will come."

The whole town **applauded** as Builda accepted her prize. "It is made from recycled material," whispered Chief. As her community clapped and cheered, Builda realized that sometimes one little idea could make a huge difference.

Discussion Questions

Name three objects in your home that you can
reuse after you are finished with them.

Tell how you would use each object in a different way.

Recycling is a form of community service.
Can you think of other ways that you can help your community?